The BIG BOOK of NONSENSE

The BIG BOOK of NONSENSE

COLIN WEST

TED SMART

First published in 2001

1 3 5 7 9 10 8 6 4 2

© Colin West 1982, 1984, 1987, 1988, 1990, 1995, 2001

Colin West has asserted his right under the Copyright,
Designs and Patents Act, 1988,
to be identified as the author and illustrator of this work

This edition produced for The Book People Ltd,
Hall Wood Avenue, Haydock, St Helens WA11 9UL

Random House Australia (Pty) Limited
20 Alfred Street, Milsons Point, Sydney
New South Wales 2061, Australia

Random House New Zealand Limited
18 Poland Road, Glenfield
Auckland 10, New Zealand

Random House South Africa (Pty) Limited
Endulini, 5A Jubilee Road, Parktown 2193, South Africa

The Random House Group Limited Reg. No. 954009

www.randomhouse.co.uk

A CIP catalogue record for this book is available from the British Library

Printed in Hong Kong
by Midas Printing Ltd

CONTENTS

Funny Folk

Curious Creatures

Tricky Tongue-twisters

Moments with Monsters

Dotty Ditties

Vicious Verses

Nothing but Nonsense

Poems to Ponder

Crazy Characters

Hopeless History

Stories in Stanzas

Ridiculous Rhymes

Foreword
by Colin West

Here are the rhymes to read to others:
Fathers, mothers, sisters, brothers;
Here are poems in their dozens
For your grannies and your cousins;
Here are tales of crazy creatures
To be read to friends and teachers;
Here are songs and here are shanties
For your uncles and your aunties;
And in this book upon your shelf
Are words to keep just for yourself.

My Sister Sybil

Sipping soup, my sister Sybil
Seems inclined to drool and dribble.
If it wasn't for this foible,
Meal-times would be more enjoible!

Mavis Morris

Mavis Morris was a girl
Who liked to pirouette and twirl.
One day upon a picnic, she
Whirled enthusiastically.
A hundred times she spun around –
And bored herself into the ground.

Ben

Ben's done something really bad.
He's forged a letter from his dad.
He's scrawled:

> Dear Miss,
>
>   Please let Ben be
> Excused this week of all P.E.
> He's got a bad cold in his chest
> And so I think it might be best
> If he ~~threwout~~ ~~throo~~ throughout
>   this week could be
> Excused from doing all P.E.
>
> I hope my ~~righting~~ writing's
>   not too bad.
>
>   Yours sincerely,
>   (signed)
>   Ben's Dad.

My Obnoxious Brother Bobby

My obnoxious brother Bobby
Has a most revolting hobby;
There, behind the garden wall is
Where he captures creepy-crawlies.

Grannies, aunts and baby cousins
Come to our house in their dozens,
But they disappear discreetly
When they see him smiling sweetly.

For they know, as he approaches,
In his pockets are cockroaches,
Spiders, centipedes and suchlike;
All of which they do not much like.

As they head towards the lobby,
Bidding fond farewells to Bobby,
How they wish he'd change his habits
And keep guinea pigs or rabbits.

But their wishes are quite futile,
For he thinks that bugs are cute. I'll
Finish now, but just remind you:
Bobby could be right behind you!

In One Ear and Out the Other

When Miss Tibbs talks
To my dear brother,
It goes in one ear
And out the other;
And when she shouts,
He seldom hears,
The words just whistle
Through his ears.

His ears are big,
(You must've seen 'em)
But he's got nothing
In between 'em.
The truth, Miss Tibbs,
Is hard to face:
His head is full
Of empty space.

Uncle Fred

My Uncle Fred,
He went to bed,
He went to sleep
And dreamt he
Drank from a cup –
And waking up,
The goldfish bowl
Was empty.

An Alphabet of Horrible Habits

A is for
Albert who
makes lots of
noise

B is for Bertha
who bullies
the boys

C is for
Cuthbert who
teases the cat

D is for Dilys
whose singing
is flat

E is for Enid
who's never
on time

F is for
Freddy who's
covered in
slime

G is for
Gilbert who
never says
thanks

H is for
Hannah who
plans to rob
banks

I is for Ivy
who slams the
front door

J is for Jacob
whose jokes
are a bore

K is for
Kenneth who
won't wash his
face

L is for Lucy
who cheats in
a race

M is for Maurice who gobbles his food

N is for Nora who runs about nude

O is for Olive who treads on your toes

Q is for Queenie who won't tell the truth

P is for Percy who *will* pick his nose

R is for Rupert who's rather uncouth

S is for Sibyl who bellows and bawls

T is for Thomas who scribbles on walls

U is for Una who fidgets too much

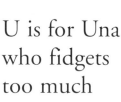

V is for Victor who talks double Dutch

W is for Wilma who won't wipe her feet

Y is for Yorick who's vain as can be

X is for Xerxes who never is neat

and Z is for Zoe who doesn't love me.

Norman Norton's Nostrils

Oh, Norman Norton's nostrils
Are powerful and strong;
Hold on to your belongings
If he should come along.

And do not ever let him
Inhale with all his might,
Or else your pens and pencils
Will disappear from sight.

Right up his nose they'll vanish;
Your future will be black.
Unless he gets the sneezes
You'll *never* get them back!

When Betty Eats Spaghetti

When Betty eats spaghetti,
She slurps, she slurps, she slurps,
And when she's finished slurping,
She burps, she burps, she burps.

My Sister Joan

I'm sad to say my sister Joan
Has confiscated my trombone,
And so, to get my *own* back,
Tonight, as she's tucked up in bed,
I'll play my violin instead …
Till I get my trombone back.

Knitting

She tried to knit a nightcap,
She tried to knit a scarf,
She tried to knit a cardigan,
Too big, they were, by half.

She tried to knit a waistcoat,
She tried to knit a shawl,
She tried to knit a bobble hat:
They all turned out too small.

And now she's knitting knickers,
And if *they* do not fit,
We'll make her wear them anyhow
Until she's learned to knit …

Deborah, Deborah

Deborah, Deborah, Deborah is it
Possible for you to visit
Far-off lands that are exquisite,
And though I wouldn't *force* you,
I hear the Outer Hebrides
Are beautiful, so Deborah please,
Ride off upon my zebra, he's
Just waiting for a horseshoe!

Mary, the Mixed-up Mermaid

Now, once upon a time there was a mermaid
Who looked just like her sisters of the sea,
Above her tummy button being human,
Below it being fishy as can be.

But Mary was a restless sort of mermaid,
Who didn't care for salty spray or foam,

She longed to live beside a yellow cornfield
Upon a hill, where she might feel at home.

Each night she slept beneath the dancing moonbeams,
And dreamed of picking pears and climbing trees;
She dreamed of doing cartwheels in the clover,
And keeping seven hives of honey bees.

One day upon the rocks she sat daydreaming,
When suddenly an octopus appeared.
To her amazement, up it crawled beside her,
And whispered words which sounded rather weird.

It said, "Galumph! Begorra! and Bedraggle!"
It said, "Balloo! Hooray! and Jamboree!"
It then arose, and with a funny totter,
It wibble-wobbled back into the sea.

Galumph! Begorra! BALLOO! Jamboree! Bedraggle! HOORAY!

I can't say what those words meant that it mumbled,
But somehow Mary seemed to understand.
From that day on, she swims around contented,
And dreams no more of living on the land.

Clumsy Clarissa

Clarissa did the washing up:
She smashed a plate and chipped a cup,
And dropped a glass and cracked a mug,
Then pulled the handle off a jug.
She couldn't do much worse, you'd think,
But then she went and broke the sink.

Adolphus

Adolphus is despicable –
Before the day begins,
To prove that I am kickable,
He kicks me in the shins.

Tout Ensemble

Paula pounds the grand piano,
Vera plays the violin,
Percival provides percussion
On an empty biscuit tin.
Connie plays the concertina,
Mervyn strums the mandolin;
When you put them all together –
They make one almighty din.

Nora the Nibbler

Nora nibbles like a rabbit,
It's a funny sort of habit.
First a carrot she will pick up,
Nibble it, then start to hiccup,
After which she'll start to nibble
Once more at her vegetibble.

O That Ogre!

O that Ogre,
In a toga,
Doing yoga
On my lawn!
What a prancer,
What a stancer,
Fattest dancer
Ever born!
Watch him tumble,
Feel him fumble,
Hear him mumble
On till dawn:
"I'm an Ogre
In a toga,
Doing yoga
On your lawn!"

Lanky Lee and Lindy Lou

Said Lanky Lee
To Lindy Lou,
"Please let me run
Away with you!"
But Lou replied
With frustration:
"You've got no
Imagination,
For that is all,
Dear Lanky Lee,
That ever runs
Away with *me*!"

Muriel

Muriel, Muriel,
You're oh so mercurial,
One moment you're up,
The next moment you're down.
Your moods are not durable,
You seem quite incurable –
For now you are laughing,
But soon you will frown.

Joe

We don't mention Joe
In this house any more;
No, not since he nailed
Mother's boots to the floor.
What makes matters worse
With regard to this crime
Is Mother was wearing
Her boots at the time.

Percy the Pirate

When people think of pirates,
They think of strapping men
With cutlasses and whiskers,
And names like Jake or Ben.

But Percy was a pirate
More fearsome than the rest,
Although he had no muscles
Or hairs upon his chest.

For Percy's secret weapon
No brute could ever beat,

He never was without it –
His pair of smelly feet.

When he was out marauding,
His foes he would out-fox
By rapidly removing
His boots, and then his socks.

And then he'd do a handstand
And wave his feet aloft,
And so upon the ozone
The whiff would gently waft.

His victims' eyes would water,
Their noses, they would sniff,

Then forcefully the fellows
Would catch the pungent whiff.

And falling down like nine-pins,
They'd all be knocked out cold,
Then Percy would relieve them
Of jewellery and gold.

Yes, Percy was the pirate
No brute could ever beat,
Who owned a ton of treasure
Thanks solely to his feet.

Nicola

I'm glad I'm not
Like Nicola,
Who may look sweet
As honey.
But even if you
Tickle her,
She doesn't find
It funny.

Winifred

Why do you do it,
Winifred?
Why do you stand
Upon your head?
Why don't you stand
Upon your feet,
Like everybody
Else I meet?
Does standing up
That way instead
Ensure you keep
A level head?
Is *that* the reason,
Winifred?

Cousin Jack

My cousin Jack
And his pet yak
Took off to Katmandu.

(Boo hoo!)

Now if that yak
Don't soon come back,
I'll have to go there too.

Veronica

Adventurous Veronica
Upon her yacht *Japonica*
Is sailing to Dominica.
She blows her old harmonica
Each night beneath the
     spinnaker,
And dreams of seeing Monica,
Her sister, in Dominica.

Curious Creatures

Our Hippopotamus

We thought a lively pet to keep
Might be a hippopotamus.
Now see him sitting in a heap,
And notice at the bottom – us.

The Tortoise

The tortoise has a tendency
To live beyond his prime,
Thus letting his descendants see
How *they* will look in time.

The Scorpion

Spiders, scorpions and mites
Are not the pleasantest of sights;
The scorpion, especially,
Does not endear itself to me.
Yet, looks aside, I must confess,
If ever I'm about to dress,
And notice one inside my shoe,
It's not as bad as failing to.

A Penguin's Life

A penguin's life is cold and wet
And always in a muddle,
A penguin's feet are wet and damp
And often in a puddle.

O how ironic! O how absurd!
A penguin cannot fly about
Like any other bird.
O how monotonous,
I'd so much like to be
A big fat hippopotamus
Upon the rolling sea!

A penguin's nose is frozen stiff
And feels just like an icicle,
A penguin has to be content
To live without a bicycle.

O how ironic! O how absurd!
That I'm not supersonic
Like any other bird.
O the frustration,
I'd so much like to hear
The trains at Tooting Station
And the trams at Belvedere!

Good Homes for Kittens

Who'd like a Siamese?
Yes, please.

An Angora?
I'd adora.

A Tabby?
Ma'be.

A Black and White?
All right.

A Tortoiseshell?
Oh, very well.

A Manx?
No thanx!

The Grizzly Bear

The grizzly bear is horrible,
His habits quite deplorable.
He's not the sort of beast
I'd ask to tea.
The reason for my quibble is
I think *Ursus horribilis*
Looks just the sort of beast
Who might eat *me*.

Glow-worm

I know a worried glow-worm,
I wonder what the matter is?
He seems so glum and gloomy,
Perhaps he needs new batteries!

The Goldfish

The goldfish swimming in its bowl
May seem a rather lonely soul,
But better that than being in
An overcrowded sardine tin.

Old Shivermetimbers

Old Shivermetimbers, the Sea-faring Cat,
Was born on the edge of the ocean,
And his days (just to prove that the world isn't flat)
Are spent in perpetual motion.

Old Shivermetimbers, the Nautical Cat,
Has seen every port of the atlas;
First feline, he was, to set foot in Rabat,
A place which was hitherto catless.

Old Shivermetimbers, the Sea-faring Cat,
Has numbered as seventy-seven
The times that he's chartered the cold Kattegat
And steered by the stars up in Heaven.

Old Shivermetimbers, the Nautical Cat,
Loves the scent of the sea on his whiskers,
So it isn't surprising to hear him say that
He don't give a hoot for hibiscus.

Old Shivermetimbers, the Sea-faring Cat,
Has travelled aboard the *Queen Mary*,
Though I saw him last Saturday queuing up at
Calais, for the cross-Channel ferry.

Old Shivermetimbers, the Nautical Cat,
Has spent his whole life on the ocean,
Yet how he acquired that old admiral's hat,
I honestly haven't a notion.

The Pig

The table manners of the pig
Leave much to be desired.
His appetite is always big,
His talk is uninspired.

And if you ask him out to dine
You'll only ask him once,
Unless you like to see a swine
Who gobbles as he grunts.

The Crab

The crab has still far to evolve
Till he attains perfection,
For still, it seems, he cannot solve
The question of direction.
So when he goes from "A" to "B"
Along the ocean tideways,
He also visits "C" and "D"
Because he travels sideways!

The Polar Bear

In Arctic lands the polar bear
Is anything but svelte.
He lies about throughout the year,
And only has one nagging fear:
He hopes the sun will not appear
In case the ice should melt.

The Bat

The bat in flight at dead of night
Can flap about with ease,
For with his ears he somehow steers
A path between the trees.

Flamingoes

Flamingoes are a shocking pink,
With just one leg to stand on.
The other leg they use, I think,
To practise how to land on.

Octopus

Last Saturday I came across
Most nonchalant an octopus;
I couldn't help but make a fuss,
And shook him by the tentacle.

He seemed to find it all a bore
And asked me, "Have we met before?
I'm sorry, but I can't be sure,
You chaps all look identical."

Auntie Agnes's Cat

My Auntie Agnes has a cat.
I do not like to tell her that
Its body seems a little large
(With lots of stripes for camouflage).
Its teeth and claws are also larger
Than they ought to be. A rajah
Gave her the kitten, I recall,
When she was stationed in Bengal.
But that was many years ago,
And kittens are inclined to grow.
So now she has a fearsome cat –
But I don't like to tell her that.

Chameleons

Chameleons are seldom seen,
They're red, they're orange, then they're green.
They're one of nature's strangest sights,
Their colours change like traffic lights!

Anteater

Pray, have you met my nice new pet,
An anteater is he,
There's just one hitch – I'm apt to itch
When serving up his tea.

The Sloth

The sloth may smile,
The sloth may frown.
It's hard to tell –
He's upside down!

Proboscis Monkey

Proboscis monkey, I suppose
You've grown accustomed to your nose.
But what precisely did you do
To get that nose to grow on you?

Geraldine Giraffe

The
longest
ever
woolly
scarf
was
worn
by
Geraldine
Giraffe.
Around
her
neck
the
scarf
she
wound,
but
still
it
trailed
upon
the
ground.

Pangolin

This disrespectful pangolin
Reclines upon a pillow,
And plays upon a mandolin
Made from an armadillo.

To sing his songs is his intent,
At nineteen to the dozen,
And so he strums an instrument
That used to be his cousin.

The Oyster

The oyster, he is
Quite extraordinary:
The moister he is,
The more he is merry.

The Auk

How very awkward for the auk
To be resigned to merely squawk,
And never say a single word
To anyone but fellow bird.

And yet, supposing we could teach
The auk the art of human speech,
If we should ever ask him out,
Whatever would we talk about?

Moose

What use
a moose?

Except, perhaps,
for coats and caps.

The Orang-utan

The closest relative of man
They say, is the orang-utan;
And when I look at Grandpapa,
I realize how right they are.

O Rattlesnake, Rattlesnake

O Rattlesnake, Rattlesnake,
What noise does your rattle make?
O won't you please rattle
Your rattle for me?

(So the Rattlesnake rattled its rattle.)

O Rattlesnake, Rattlesnake,
Pray, doesn't your rattle ache?
You've rattled your rattle
Since twenty to three.

(Still the Rattlesnake rattled its rattle.)

O Rattlesnake, Rattlesnake,
Please no more your rattle shake.
O won't you stop rattling
Your rattle, pray do!

(But the Rattlesnake rattled its rattle.)

O Rattlesnake, Rattlesnake,
For you and your rattle's sake,
You'd better stop rattling
Your rattle. Thank you!

(So the Rattlesnake bit me instead.)

The Paradoxical Leopard

The spots the leopard's
Been allotted
Are there so leopards
Can't be spotted.

Tricky Tongue-twisters

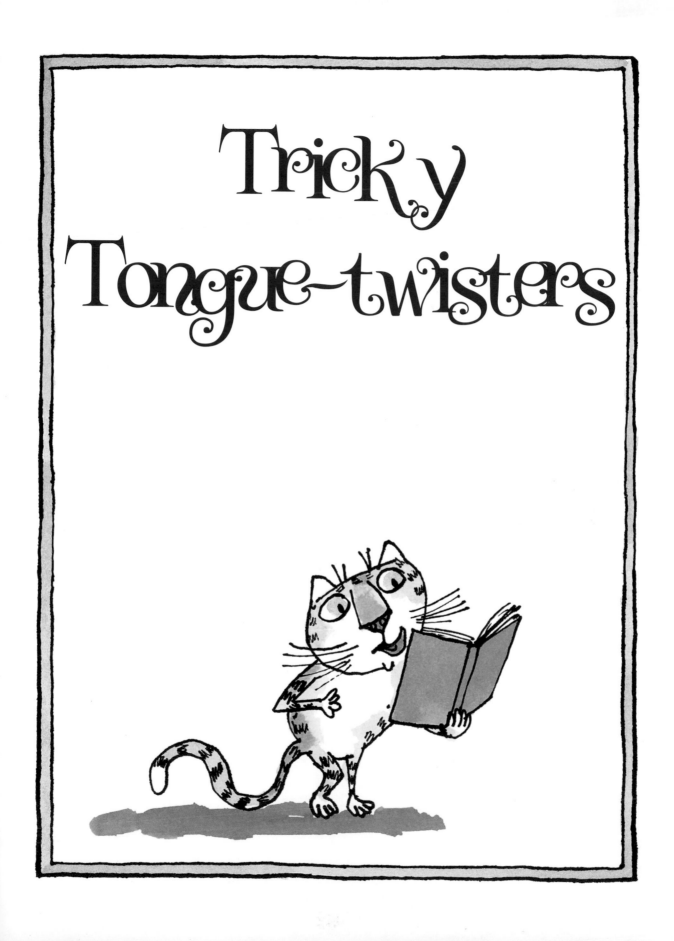

Willoughby the Wallaby

I want to be a wallaby,
A wallaby like Willoughby,
When *will* I be a wallaby
Like Willoughby the wallaby?

Cynthia Smith

Cynthia Smith has still not thought
A single thought since Thursday,
Since Cynthia Smith is not the sort
To think a single sort of thought.

Kitty and the Kittiwake

Did Kitty wake
The kittiwake,
Or did the kittiwake
Wake Kitty?

Adelaide

Adelaide is up a ladder.
Adelaide's an adder-upper.
She's an addled adder-upper,
Adding adders up a ladder.

Passers-by

A passer-by
Was passing by
A by-pass,
And passing by
The by-pass,
A passer-by
Passed by:
By passing by
A by-pass
As a passer-by.
Passed by,
A passer-by
Was passed by
By a by-pass
Passer-by.

When Jilly eats Jelly

When Jilly eats jelly,
Then Jilly is jolly.
But melons make Melanie
Most melancholy.

Canoe

I can't canoe my old canoe,
I need a new canoe.
Can you canoe my old canoe
And I'll canoe the new?

Juggler Jim

I'm Jim and I juggle a jug and a jar
And junkets and jelly and jam.
With jovial, joyful and jocular jests,
How jolly a jester I am!

Please Pass the Parsley, Percival

Please pass the parsley, Percival,
Please pass the parsley, Percy,
The parsley, Percival, please pass,
Please, Percy, pass the parsley.

If a Ghoul
is Fond of Goulash

If a ghoul is fond of goulash,
Is the ghoul, a little foolish;
Should he feel, if full of goulash,
As a ghoul he's not so ghoulish?

King Canute Cannot

King Canute cannot k-nit,
K-nit Canute cannot;
King Canute cannot k-nit,
King Canute cannot!

Superciliousness

Some say they think that "super"
Is not the thing to say:
They say that super's silly;
Oh, supercilious they!

Beetroot

Be true to me, beetroot, be true,
And I will too be true;
But beetroot, if you be untrue,
I'll be untrue to you.

Scarecrows

The trouble with scarecrows
Is that they *don't* scare crows,
And don't seem to care crows
Are not scared by scarecrows.

Toboggan

To begin to toboggan, first buy a toboggan,
But don't buy too big a toboggan.
(A too big a toboggan is not a toboggan
To buy to begin to toboggan.)

Yo-yo

Yes, you may use my yo-yo,
My yo-yo made of yew.
My yellow yo-yo made of yew
Is yours to use in Yeovil,
And York and Yarmouth too.
Yea, use my yo-yo yonder
Till it gets used to you,
And yodel as you use it,
My yo-yo made of yew.

My Whites

I used to think my whites were white
Until I saw the whiter whites
Of Mrs White whose whiter whites
Were whiter than my whites were.

A Cymbal for the Singer

Here's a cymbal for the singer
With a thimble on his finger:
See the singer with a thimble
On his finger thump the cymbal!

Mr Lott's Allotment

Mr Lott's allotment
Meant a lot to Mr Lott.
Now Mr Lott is missed a lot
On Mr Lott's allotment.

Nutpickers

Who nicked the nuts
That the nutpickers picked
When the nutpickers
Picked their nuts?

The picnickers nicked
The nutpickers' nuts
When the nutpickers
Picked their nuts.

Ethel Read a Book

Ethel read, Ethel read,
Ethel read a book.
Ethel read a book in bed,
She read a book on Ethelred.
The book that Ethel read in bed,
(The book on Ethelred) was red.
The book was red that Ethel read,
In bed on Ethelred.

Moments
with
Monsters

The Flipper-Flopper Bird

O have you never ever heard
Of the Flipper-Flopper Bird?
O have you never seen his teeth,
Two above and one beneath?

O have you never known the thrill
Of stroking his enormous bill?
O have you never taken tea
With him sitting up a tree?

O have you never seen him hop
As he goes a-flip, a-flop?
O have you never heard his cry?
No, you've never? Nor have I.

The Ogglewop

The Ogglewop is tall and wide,
And though he looks quite passive,
He's crammed with boys and girls inside,
That's why he is so massive!

The Blunderblat

Until I saw the Blunderblat
I doubted its existence;
But late last night with Vera White,
I saw one in the distance.

I reached for my binoculars,
Which finally I focused;
I watched it rise into the skies,
Like some colossal locust.

I heard it hover overhead,
I shrieked as it came nearer;
I held my breath, half scared to death,
And prayed it might take Vera.

And so it did, I'm glad to say,
Without too much resistance.
Dear Blunderblat, I'm sorry that
I doubted your existence.

The Thinkalot

Of all the things I'm glad I'm not
There's one thing in particular –
I'm glad I'm not a Thinkalot
Or *Pondus perpendicular*.

The Thinkalot can stand up straight,
His head is almost spherical,
But vain attempts to find a mate
Have driven him hysterical.

He gabbles at the first excuse
And seems quite intellectual,
But is, in fact, of little use,
His brain is ineffectual.

The Furbelow

The Furbelow will eat your home,
From the floorboards to the rafters;
Then, having scoffed the furniture,
Will eat you up for afters.

The Finisher-Upper

To demolish a dinner
Or diminish a supper,
Why don't you call for
The Finisher-Upper?

Watch him demolish
And watch him diminish
Any old left-over food
He can finish.

His performance is always
So perfect and polished:
Suppers diminished
And dinners demolished!

The Glump

Your life may be in jeopardy,
The Glump is on its way.
Its legs are long and leopardy,
It pounces on its prey.

It bears some similarity,
You'll notice, to a bird.
Its beak is pink and parroty,
Its cry is quite absurd.

I think the Glump is easily
Our most obnoxious beast.
Its teeth are white and weaselly,
And waiting for a feast.

You'll reel and writhe in agony,
Unless you disappear.
Its skin is dry and dragony …
Oh dear, the Glump is here.

The Neither-One-Thing-Nor-Another

The Neither-One-Thing-Nor-Another
Is neither round nor square,
Has neither hide nor hair,
Can neither do nor dare.

The Neither-One-Thing-Nor-Another
Is neither foul nor fair,
Goes neither dressed nor bare,
Can neither growl nor glare.

The Neither-One-Thing-Nor-Another
Has gone to Who-Knows-Where,
But no one seems to care,
It's neither here nor there.

Monstrous Imagination

"Mummy, can't you see the monster
Hiding by the curtain?"
"Why Joseph dear, there's nothing there,
Of that I am quite certain.
The monster that you *think* you see
Within the shadows lurking,
Is your imagination, dear,
Which overtime is working."

Thus reassured, Joe went to sleep;
His mother's explanation
Seemed only right: Beasts of the Night
Are mere imagination.
And sound his slumber was until
In dreams the monster met him.
Now Joe we'll miss, for last night his
"Imagination" ate him.

Dotty Ditties

Pretty Polly Perkins

"Pretty Polly Perkins,
What would you like to eat?
Greengages and gherkins,
Or marmalade and meat?

Cakes and Coca-Cola,
Or chocolate and ham?
Grapes and Gorgonzola,
Or sausages and jam?"

"Thank you sir," says Polly,
"But what would please me most
Would be a lemon lolly
Upon a slice of toast."

The Trouble with Boys

The trouble with boys is
They make funny noises;
They rage and they riot,
And seldom are quiet.
They seem extra naughty
With folk over forty,
And do things they oughtn't
To persons important.

Dressing Gown

Why do people
I'm addressing
Frown
When I've got on
My dressing
Gown?
And some give me
A dressing
Down
When I've got on
My dressing
Gown?

The Hole Truth

If it takes three men to dig one hole
Two hours and one minute,
How long would six men take to dig
A hole exactly twice as big,
And could you push them in it?

Pogo Stick

Upon my pogo stick I pounce
And out of school I homeward bounce.
I bounce so high, how my heart pounds
Until at last I'm out of bounds.

Amongst My Friends

Amongst my friends
I number some
Sixteen or so
Who dance.
Some like to do
The rhumba, some
Will waltz if they've
The chance;
And even in their slumber, some
Will foxtrot in
A trance.
But as for me,
I'm cumbersome,
And all I do
Is prance.

The Loofah

The loofah feels he can't relax,
For something is amiss:
He scratches other people's backs,
But no one scratches *his*.

What do Teachers Dream of?

What do teachers dream of,
In mountains and in lowlands?
They dream of exclamation marks,
Full stops and semi-colons!

Putting the Shot

Tomorrow I may put the shot,
Or on the other hand, may not;
For yesterday I put the shot,
But where I put it, I forgot.

Luke

Luke's a lisper.
I've heard a whisper,
He's at his zenith
Playing tennith.

Custard

I like it thin without a skin,
My sister likes it thicker.
But thick or thin, when tucking in,
I'm noisier and quicker.

Sabre-toothed Tigers

It's pointless being polite
If sabre-toothed tigers attack;
So if they're beginning to bite,
Be bold for a bit and bite back.

My Auntie

My auntie who lives in
Llanfairpwllgwyngyllgogerych-
  wyrndrobwllllantysiliogogogoch
Has asked me to stay.

But unfortunately
Llanfairpwllgwyngyllgogerych-
  wyrndrobwllllantysiliogogogoch
Is a long, long way away.

Will I ever go to
Llanfairpwllgwyngyllgogerych-
  wyrndrobwllllantysiliogogogoch?
It's difficult to say.

Bed of Nails

I sleep upon a bed of nails.
I must confess it never fails
To help me get a good night's rest,
And, overall, I'm most impressed!

A Pelican in Delhi Can

A pelican in Delhi can
Spend his whole life alone.
But an elephant in Delhi can't
Be often on his own.

Orange Silver Sausage

Some words I've studied for a time,
Like *orange, silver, sausage*;
But as for finding them a rhyme,
I'm at a total lossage.

Snakes and Ladders

Up the rungs and
down the adders
Life's a game of
Snakes and Ladders.

Petunia's Pet

Petunia's pet is a pet-and-a-half,
Some say it's a tapir, some say a giraffe.
Some say it is neither, some say it is both,
But Pet doesn't care and she's plighted her troth.

Fungus

It's most fantastic fun to be a fungus,
But no one seems to care for us a lot;
So for revenge, the mischievous among us
Look edible, but actually are not.

Trampoline

I'm sorry to disturb you, miss, I hate to intervene,

But could you for a moment, please, put down your magazine?

I've got a hundred pounds to spend, and I am really keen,

If you could only serve me, miss, to buy this trampoline.

Insides

I'm very grateful to my skin
For keeping all my insides in –
I do so hate to think about
What I would look like inside-out.

Nowhere-in-Particular

O, Nowhere-in-Particular
Is just the place for me,
I go there every now and then
For two weeks or for three.

And Doing Nothing Special there
Is what I like to do,
At Nowhere-in-Particular
For three weeks or for two.

Penfriend

The letters that
Sue-Ellen sends
Come all the way
From Texas;
And now we're more
Than just penfriends,
For when she signs
Her name, she tends
To add, "with lots
Of love" and ends
With loads and loads
Of X's.

Hedgehog's Valentine

If you're sickly,
Feeling prickly,
As your trickly
Tears fall thickly,
Don't act fickly,
Kiss me quickly,
You'll feel tickly,
Not so prickly,
And partickly
Far from sickly.

French Accents

Acute, or Grave or Circumflex,
In France we use all three;
And sometimes too, Cedilla who
Is found beneath the C.

Uncle Harry

My Uncle Harry
had a horse,

But kept on
falling off it.

We charged a
pound to come
and watch,

And made a
handsome profit.

Auntie Dotty

My Auntie Dotty thought it nice
To twirl about upon the ice.
I warned her persons of proportions
Such as hers, should take precautions,
But poor Auntie was so fond
Of skating on the village pond,
That she took no heed of warning
And went skating every morning.

Now we mourn for Auntie Dot:
The ice was thin, but she was not.

When Rover Passed Over

When Rover died, my sister cried;
I tried my best to calm her.
I said, "We'll have him mummified,
I know a good embalmer."

And so we packed the wretched pup
Into a wicker basket.
We duly had him bandaged up,
And kept him in a casket.

Now Rover we will not forget,
Though he is but a dummy,
For though we've lost a faithful pet,
We've gained an extra Mummy!

Percy and the Python

Poor Percy met a python once
When walking in the jungle,
And being something of a dunce,
He made a fatal bungle.

He went to stroke its scaly skin
As from a tree it dangled,
Alas, before he could begin,
The python left him strangled.

It then went on to crush to pulp
His body, very neatly;
Until, with one enormous gulp,
It swallowed him completely.

This story shows that such a snake
Should always be avoided,
So do not make the same mistake
As this unthinking boy did.

Betty

Wearing all her diamonds, Betty
Rode too fast along the jetty.
How I wish she'd not been reckless;
We could not retrieve her necklace.

Kitty

Isn't it a
Dreadful pity
What became of
Dreamy Kitty,
Noticing the
Moon above her,
Not
   the
      missing
        man-hole
          cover?

Misguided Marcus

Marcus met an alligator
Half a mile from the equator;
Marcus, ever optimistic,
Said, "This beat is not sadistic,"
Marcus even claimed the creature
"Has a kind and loving nature."
In that case, pray tell me, Marcus,
Why have you become a carcass?

Archibald's Progress

Archibald liked pulling faces,
All day long he'd make grimaces,
And at school he'd taunt his teachers
With contortions of his features.

Sitting at his school desk smugly,
Once he pulled a face so ugly,
That he gave poor Miss McKenzie
Cause to fly into a frenzy:

Mouth wide open – how revolting!
Tongue protruding – how insulting!
Puffed-out cheeks and wrinkled forehead –
Archibald looked really horrid!

Thus it was the nasty creature
So provoked his gentle teacher,
That she, driven to distraction,
Took at once most drastic action.

Pelting him with books, she dented
Archie's head till he repented,
And agreed that when at places
Such as school, he'd not pull faces.

Let us now praise Miss McKenzie,
She who flew into a frenzy,
And in just one scripture session,
Made a permanent impression.

Aunt Carol

Making vinegar, Aunt Carol
Fell into her brimming barrel.
As she drowned, my teardrops trickled;
Now she's permanently pickled.

Kate

In the kitchen Kate went tripping
Landing in a vat of dripping.
When the Red Cross came to fetch her,
Kate kept slipping off the stretcher.

Septimus

From the mountain's dizzy summit
Septimus is soon to plummet.
This, alas, will prove the last time
He goes climbing as a pastime.

Auntie Babs

Auntie Babs became besotted
With her snake, so nicely spotted,
Unaware that pets so mottled
Like to leave their keepers throttled.

Cousin Jane

Yesterday my cousin Jane
Said she was an aeroplane,
But I wanted further proof
So I pushed her off the roof.

Malcolm

Let us pray for cousin Malcolm,
Smothered as he was in talcum;
He sneezed whilst seasoning his chowder
And vanished in a puff of powder.

Laurence

Laurence by a lion was mauled,
And it's left us quite appalled.
He had on his "Sunday best";
Now he's gone and torn his vest.

Little Barbara

Little Barbara went to Scarborough,
Just to buy a candelabra.
At the harbour a bear ate Barbara.
Don't you find that most macabre?

Nothing but Nonsense

The Cat and the King

A cat may look at a king
And a king may look at a cat.
If thin the cat and fat the king,
There isn't much danger in *that*.
But just suppose fat is the cat,
Conversely, thin the king,
The king gets mighty cross at that,
And stamps like anything.

Words with Teacher

These are the words that teachers use:
Hypothesis, hypotenuse,
Isosceles, trapezium,
Potassium, magnesium,
Denominator, catechism
And antidisestablishmentarianism.

An Understanding Man

I have an understanding
With an understanding man:
His umbrella I stand under
When I understand I can.

The Carpet with a Hole

Once a merchant in a market
Showed a tatty-looking carpet
To a rather foolish fellow.
It was purple, pink and yellow
With a big hole in the middle.
(Which seemed something of a fiddle!)

But this fellow still adored it,
And could just about afford it,
So he bought that tatty carpet
And he took it from the market
To a faraway oasis
(One of his most favourite places),
And that carpet with a hole in
He was presently unrollin'.
It was damp and it was dusty
And it smelled a little musty,

But to that misguided fellow
It seemed mystical and mellow;
Though the middle bit was perished,
That old carpet still he cherished,
So he thought he'd sit upon it
And compose a little sonnet
All about that tatty carpet
Which he'd purchased from the market.

(Notice how the hole is fitting
Round him, in the middle, sitting.)

Holey rug, you have a beauty
Far beyond the call of duty …
Thus he scribbled with his biro.
Meanwhile, somewhere south of Cairo,
There appeared a change of weather:
Little breezes blew together
And in strength they started growing
Till one mighty blast was blowing …

Over rooftops, over fountains,
Over deserts, over mountains,
It came swishing, it came swooshing,
It came whishing, it came whooshing,
Bending trees and blowing camels
Off their feet, the poor old mammals.

Who'd have thought a breeze on high would
Sweep that holey carpet skyward?
But it did – with one great bluster
Up it went! Just like a duster
High above, the carpet fluttered!
Back on earth the fellow muttered:
"Mercy me! It's truly tragic,
For that carpet's clearly magic,
I'd be flying single-handed
If it hadn't left me stranded.
I'd be swooping like a swallow
If that rug had not been hollow,
But as I composed my idyll,
I was sitting in the middle –
Where that hole was all around me –
Such calamities confound me!"

As he spoke, the carpet vanished,
And to Who-Knows-Where was banished.

No more did he see that carpet.
Did it blow back to the market?
Was it on a secret mission?
Was the merchant some magician?
Did the hole have mystic powers?
One could contemplate for hours
What became of that old carpet
Which was purchased in the market;
But that carpet in whose middle
Was a hole, remains a riddle.

Sports

Playing tennis,
I'm no menace.
As for croquet,
I'm just "OK".

Then there's cricket –
Can't quite lick it.
Ditto: rowing,
Discus-throwing.

Also: biking,
Jogging, hiking,
Ten-pin bowling,
And pot-holing.

Can't play hockey.
I'm no jockey,
Daren't go riding,
Or hang-gliding.

Nor can I jump
Long or high jump.
Being sporty
Ain't my forté.

I'm pathetic,
Unathletic,
But at dinner…
I'm a winner!

The Prize Pumpkin

They seized it, they squeezed it,
They gave it funny looks,
They teased it, they eased it,
They looked it up in books.
They tethered it, they weathered it,
They even tarred and feathered it,
And when they could, they measured it,
(It came to seven foot).

They gave it a prod,
They gave it a poke,
They sang it a song,
They told it a joke.

They ran to it, they walked to it,
They then began to talk to it.
They lathered it (they rathered it
Was clean as it could be).
They smothered it, they mothered it,
They fathered and they brothered it,
They watered it, they daughtered it,
And sat it on their knee.

They gave it a slap,
They gave it a punch,
They cut it in bits
And had it for lunch!

Jingle–Jangle–Jent

A Viking liking hiking walked
From Katmandu to Kent,
And Timbuctoo and Teddington
Were towns he did frequent,
And yet with everything he saw
And everywhere he went,
He never ever saw the sight
Of Jingle-Jangle-Jent;
He *never* ever saw the sight
Of Jingle-Jangle-Jent.

A Druid fond of fluid drank
More than you've ever dreamt,
It took one hundred pints of beer
Until he was content,
And yet with all the liquid that
He to his stomach sent,
He never ever knew the taste
Of Jingle-Jangle-Jent;
He *never* ever knew the taste
Of Jingle-Jangle-Jent.

A vet who let his pet get wet
In Ancient Egypt spent
His life with sickly squawks and squeals,
To which his ears he lent.
He learned what every whimper was,
What every mumble meant,
And yet he never heard the noise
Of Jingle-Jangle-Jent;
He *never* ever heard the noise
Of Jingle-Jangle-Jent.

A Roman roamin' round in Rome
Aromas did invent,
By mixing potions in a pot,
As over it he bent.
His nostrils were of noble nose,
Yet it is evident,
He never ever caught the whiff
Of Jingle-Jangle-Jent;
He *never* ever caught the whiff
Of Jingle-Jangle-Jent.

The Wherefore and the Why

The Therefore and the Thereupon,
The Wherefore and the Why;
The Hitherto, the Whitherto,
The Thus, the Thence, the Thy.

The Whysoever, Whereupon,
The Whatsoever, Whence;
The Hereinafter, Hereupon,
The Herebefore and Hence.

The Thereby and the Thereabouts,
The Thee, the Thou, the Thine;
I don't care for their whereabouts,
And they don't care for mine!

To be a Bee?

To be a bee or not to be
A bee, that is the question.
You see, I'm in a quandary.
"To be a bee or not to be
A bee" is what perplexes me,
Pray, what is your suggestion?
To be a bee or not to be
A bee, that is the question.

Longwindedness and What it Boils Down to

Would you kindly care to join me
In a game of table tennis?
(For it will be so exciting,
"Dorothea versus Dennis".)
Can we sing *O Sole Mio*
Like the gondoliers in Venice?
Dare we watch a monster movie
All about an apelike menace?

Let's watch *King Kong*, have a ding-dong
Game of ping-pong and a sing-song.

Tomorrow I've Given Up Hope

I've sailed all the seas in a bathtub,
And climbed all the mountains with rope,
I've flown in the skies
With soap in my eyes,
But tomorrow I've given up hope.

I've picked all the world's rarest flowers,
And seen the uncommonest trees,
I've paddled in ponds,
And made friends with fronds,
But tomorrow still quite eludes me.

I never have *seen* a tomorrow,
I've never been able to say:
"Tomorrow has come,
The bumblebees hum,
Tomorrow's come early today!"

Where Raindrops Plop

Where raindrops plop in muddy streams,
And thunder shakes the trees,
Where pigs who've played in football teams
Go home in twos and threes;
Where harpists pluck at mournful strings,
And sadness fills the air,
Where creep a hundred hairy things,
I think that I'll go there.

Where green leaves lie upon the lakes,
And gentle mists descend,
Where noises that the hedgehog makes
Seem only to offend;
Where darkness hangs above the fields,
And moles are made to roam,
Where stands the sett the badger builds,
That's where I'll call my home.

The Good, the Bored and the Ugly

A coachload of pupils
Get into their places –
The ones in the back seats
Make ugly grimaces.

The ones in the front seats
Are fairer of feature –
Directing the driver
And talking to Teacher.

The ones in the middle –
Halfway down the bus,
Just look bored and wonder,
"Oh, why all the fuss?"

Poems to Ponder

Rainbow Ship

Two dreams I've always cherished:
To sail upon the main,
And to regard a rainbow
Without a drop of rain.

That rainbow seemed elusive,
I never sailed the sea,
Until Uncle Horatio
A present gave to me:

A Ship Inside a Bottle!
Now in its glassy realm,
My little ship goes sailing,
With me stood at the helm.

And when the sun is shining
Upon the glass, I've found,
Without a single raindrop,
A rainbow's all around.

The Moon

The moon, she came in through my window,
When everyone else was asleep;
Her silvery light made everything bright
As softly she started to creep.

And once round my room the moon travelled
As over my pillow she passed,
And every dark nook and picture and book
Came under the gaze that she cast.

Then when she was through with exploring,
She left me without a "goodbye",
And when she was gone, I felt quite alone
To see her returned to the sky.

My Cat

My cat can stalk,
My cat can prance,
My cat can skip,
My cat can dance.

My cat can yawn,
My cat can purr,
My cat can preen
His silky fur.

My cat can leap,
My cat can pounce,
My cat can bound,
My cat can bounce.

My cat can taunt,
My cat can tease,
My cat can hide
In boughs of trees.

My cat can plod,
My cat can prowl,
My cat can scratch,
My cat can growl.

My cat can do
Just anything,
But catch a bird
That's on the wing.

Commonsense

If Commonsense were sold in shops,
I'd purchase me a pound:

I'd give a quarter
to Sir John,

A quarter
to Miss Brown,

A quarter to
old Algernon,

A quarter to
his hound.

And all the Commonsense left over,
I'd put it on the shelf,
Wrapped in a cotton handkerchief,
And keep it for myself.

Over the Orchard Wall

Over the orchard wall we'd go,
And Tom was always first,
For there grew cherries, plums and pears
To quench a summer thirst.
"It's pears and plums for me!" cried Tom,
And shook them from the tree,
While I picked cherries from a bough
To take to Rose-Marie.

But then one day, old Farmer Jones
Came by and caught us out,
And, as he chased us from his land,
I'm sure I heard him shout:
"Be off with you, you greedy boys,
For I've a family
Who must be fed – a wife, a son,
And daughter Rose-Marie."

My Colours

These are
My colours,
One by one:

Red –
The poppies
Where I run.

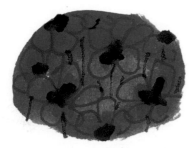

Orange –
Summer's
Setting sun.

Yellow –
Farmers'
Fields of corn.

Green –
The clover
On my lawn.

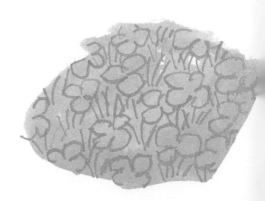

Blue –
The sea
Where fishes spawn.

Indigo –
A starling's
Feather.

Violet –
The dancing
Heather.

A rainbow
They make
All together.

The Violin-fiddle

The violin is highly strung
And melancholy is her song,
But should she choose to change her tune,
She'll fiddle 'neath a gypsy moon.

Going to the Bank

When Uncle Ben goes to the bank,
I like to go there too,
But not for business purposes
As other people do.

I go to see the blotting pad
Which on the counter lies –
For there I know I'll find a treat
On which to feast my eyes.

For everything is back to front
In Blotting Paper Land –
Men's signatures and ladies' names
Writ in a magic hand!

Mere words become weird
alphabets
Of dashes and of dots,
And who can guess what sorcery
Lies hidden in the blots?

And when I'm older, will *I* make
Strange marks on paper pink,
And leave behind *my* magic spell
In backward-slanting ink?

Shark Infested?

"These seas are shark infested,"
Said the captain to his crew.
"I beg your pardon," said a voice,
"But who invited you?"

The captain and his crew looked down,
And right beneath their noses
There swam a fearsome-looking shark
Adopting angry poses.

This passing shark
    went on to say:
"It's not as you
    suggested.
This is my
    natural habitat,
So don't say
    shark infested!"

Dodos

When dodos danced upon the sands
And welcomed men from foreign lands,
Nobody raised an eyebrow when
Those BIRDS were eaten by those MEN.
And now, because nobody blinked
An eyelid, dodos are extinct.

(How nice if we
        could switch those words,
And have the MEN
        scoffed by the BIRDS.)

The Ladybird Traveller

You've heard of a Bee in the Bonnet,
You've heard of a Fly on the Wall,
Well, I am a Ladybird Traveller,
Who travels the world at a crawl.

Frontiers for me aren't a problem,
I pass over mountains with ease,
I can stroll round the world in an hour
And cross all the Seven High Seas.

The Tropics, the Poles, the Equator,
I can visit them all in a day:
An afternoon spent in the Indies,
An evening spent in Cathay.

Africa, Asia and Europe,
My world is a peaceable place,
But should I one day find it tiresome,
I shall simply fly off into space.

The Lost Ball

My sister hit our tennis ball
Right over next door's garden wall.
Our neighbour's name is Mr Hall,
A grumpy man who's rather small.
But unlike him, his garden wall
Must stand a hundred inches tall.
It's no use to go round and call
And ask him to return our ball,
(For he's the sort who hoards each ball
Which happens on his lawn to fall).
Nor can we climb his garden wall,
And there's no gap through which to crawl.
There seems to be no chance at all
That we'll retrieve our tennis ball.
But wait, what's this? Our tennis ball!
Oh, thank you kindly, Mr Hall!

The Father Christmas on the Cake

For fifty weeks I've languished
Upon the cupboard shelf,
Forgotten and uncared for,
I've muttered to myself.
But now the year is closing,
And Christmastime is here,
They dust me down and tell me
To show a little cheer.
Between the plaster snowman
And little glassy lake
They stand me in the middle
Of some ice-covered cake,
And for a while there's laughter,
But as the week wears on,
They cut up all the landscape
Till every scrap is gone.
Then with the plaster snowman
And little lake of glass
I'm banished to the cupboard
For one more year to pass.

The Clockmaker's Shop

The clockmaker's shop is the strangest of places,
The clocks all have different times on their faces;
You never can tell if it's half past eleven
Or twenty to two or a quarter to seven.

How varied the voices of all of these clocks,
Oh, what a collection of ticketytocks!
Some with a heartbeat that seems in a flurry,
And some with a heart that refuses to hurry.

Some of them tinkle away like rain water,
And some of them strike on the dot every quarter;
Some of them sound with a simple ding-dong,
And some with a rather superior song.

Some have a sound that won't stir you in bed,
And some have alarms that could wake up the dead;
Some have a chapel-like bell of a chime,
And one has a cuckoo to tell you the time!

This House

This house, now you're away,
Misses you more each day;
Its every little room
Has its own special gloom.
The handles on the doors
Wait for a touch that's yours;
The sofa and the chairs
Long for your seat on theirs.
This house with just me in it
Misses you more each minute.

Half Measures

If I had a half a penny,
I would buy a half a loaf
And a half a pound of honey
And a half a silver knife.

Oh, I wouldn't half be happy
As the half a loaf I slice,
And I'd spread on half the honey
With my half a silver knife.

And a half of it would fill me,
And a half would fill my wife;
Oh, we wouldn't half be full up,
And it wouldn't half be nice.

But I haven't half a penny,
So I haven't half a knife,
Or a half a loaf and honey,
And I haven't half a wife.

New Term

New term,
New school,
New class,
New rules.

New desk,
New names,
New shoes,
New games.

New coat,
New hooks,
New rooms,
New books.

New bag,
New pens,
New food,
New friends.

The Incredible Cake

Oh, how shall I make
My true love a cake?
I wondered again and again.
As I didn't know,
I thought I would go
To find out the answer, so then…

"Please, how shall I make
My true love a cake?"
I asked the white horse on the hill.
He chewed the thing over,
Then answered, "With clover;
The thought of it gives me a thrill."

"And how shall I make
My true love a cake?"
I asked the red squirrel above.
He answered, "With nuts,
No ifs and no buts,
For that is the food that I love."

"And how shall I make
My true love a cake?"
I asked the brown rat in the barn.
He answered, "With grain;
To me it is plain
It's far the best stuff on the farm."

"And how shall I make
My true love a cake?"
I asked the ring dove in the wood.
He answered, "With berries,
With rosehips and cherries;
To me nothing else tastes so good."

So thinking it over,
I picked me some clover,

And no ifs and buts,
I gathered some nuts,

Then added some grain,
(The best stuff, it's plain)
And threw in some berries
With rosehips and cherries,

And I made a cake,
A wonderful cake,
Which took simply ages to bake.
But oh, what a cake,
A fabulous cake,
Which everyone helped
        me to make.

And then I did take
My true love the cake
Packed full of these goodies galore;
But soon as she bit
A mouthful of it,
I knew she would love me no more.

Yesterday, Today and Tomorrow

Yesterday I threw away
The day.
There seemed so little to be done,
And the day, it just went on and on.

Today is different,
Today
There seem so many things to do,
And the day is only halfway through.

Tomorrow, I wonder,
I wonder,
Will I throw the thing away,
Or live each moment of the day?

The Stately Ship

I sailed a ship as white as snow,
As soft as clouds on high,
Tall was the mast, broad was the
  beam,
And safe and warm was I.

I stood astern my stately ship
And felt so grand and high,
To see the lesser ships give way
As I went gliding by.

Out of Doors

An attic out of doors is a mountain,
A cellar out of doors is a cave,
A freezer out of doors is an ice block,
A washtub out of doors is a wave.

A table out of doors is a tree stump,
A carpet out of doors is a lawn,
A mattress out of doors is a haystack,
A concert out of doors is a dawn.

A mirror out of doors is a puddle,
A shower out of doors is a spa,
A painting out of doors is a sunset,
A lightbulb out of doors is a star.

Crazy Characters

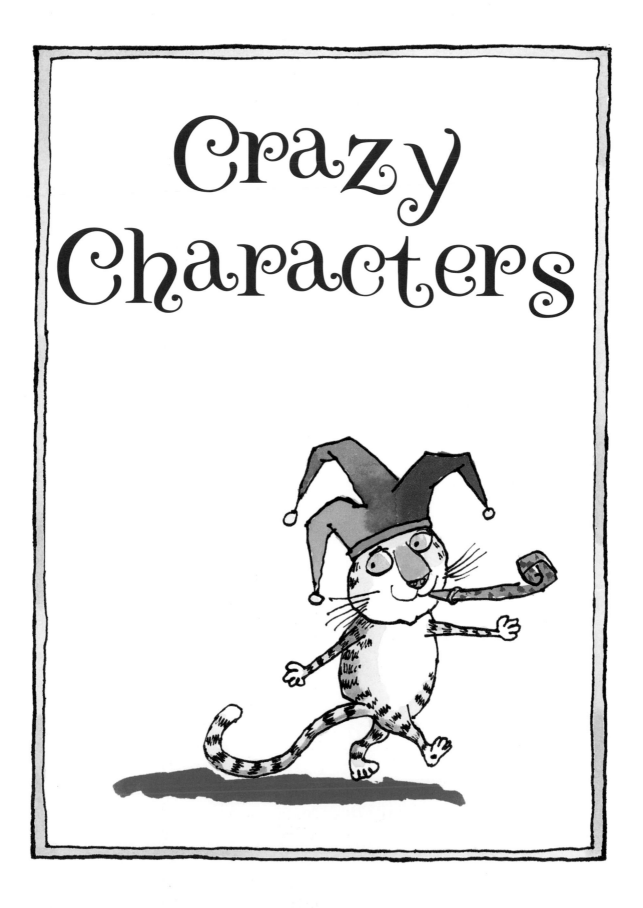

Annie and her Anaconda

Annie and her anaconda
Wander near and wander yonder.
When they wander here, I wonder
Whether Annie's anaconda
Likes it here, or is he fonder
Of the far-off places yonder?
(Where I wish *I* were, I ponder)
'Scuse me, while I grab my Honda.

The Darkest and Dingiest Dungeon

Down in the darkest and dingiest dungeon,
Far from the tiniest twinkle of stars,
Far from the whiff of a wonderful luncheon,
Far from the murmur of motoring cars,
Far from the habits of rabbits and weasels,
Far from the merits of ferrets and stoats,
Far from the danger of mumps or of measles,
Far from the fashions of fabulous coats,
Far from the turn of a screw in a socket,
Far from the fresh frozen food in the fridge,
Far from the fluff in my dufflecoat pocket,
Far from the bite of a mischievous midge,
Far from the hole in my humble umbrella,
Far from my hat as it hangs in the hall,
I sit here alone with myself in the cellar,
I *do* so like getting away from it all!

She Likes to Swim Beneath the Sea

She likes to swim beneath the sea
And wear her rubber flippers,
She likes to dance outrageously
And wake up all the kippers.

Peter

I'm not sitting next to Peter
For he's such a messy eater,
And although he's my own brother,
Can't we swap him for another?
(For I'd so prefer a sibling
Who is not forever dribbling.)

Mrs Jones

Upon her old velocipede
Comes shaky Mrs Jones,
But is that dreadful rattling
Her bicycle – or bones?

Me and Amanda

Me
and
Amanda
meander,
like
rivers
that
run
to
the
sea.
We
wander
at
random,
we're
always
in
tandem:
meandering
Mandy
and
me.

My Uncle is a Baronet

My uncle is a baronet,
He sleeps beside the hearth,
And likes to play the clarinet
Whilst sitting in the bath.

A Princess Called Pauline

There once was a princess called Pauline,
And under a tarpaulin awning
She sat on the shoreline each morning,
And spent it in stretching and yawning,
Whilst catching the crabs that were crawling
Beside her, beneath the tarpaulin.

One Sunday a fisherman trawling
For salmon nearby sighted Pauline,
And thought her the loveliest Fräulein
He'd spotted for many a morning.

He went to her tarpaulin awning
Without even giving a warning,

And said, "You appeal to me, Pauline,
Forgive me, I beg you, for calling,
But for you I'm hopelessly falling."

Still Pauline continued in yawning
And didn't acknowledge his fawning.

The fisherman, blubbing and bawling,
Returned to the business of trawling,
As Pauline, with manners appalling,
Went back to the crabs that were crawling
Beside her, beneath the tarpaulin.

Dirty Cowboy Bert

Now, here's the tale of Cowboy Bert,
Who liked to roll around in dirt,
And never washed, or changed his shirt.

Whenever Bert went into town,
The people looked him up and down,
His dirty habits made them frown.

"Of all the cowboys in the West,
I surely am the dirtiest,
I'm much more dirty than the rest!"
Sang Dirty Cowboy Bert.

But then one day, when rolling round
Upon the dirty desert ground,
Of horses' hooves he heard the sound.

And looking up, what did he see?
The sheriff and his deputy,
Complete with posse one, two, three.

Bert didn't get the chance to run,
The sheriff calmly pulled a gun,
As did the others, one by one,
On Dirty Cowboy Bert.

They fired, when having taken aim,
But from their guns no bullets came,
For it was all a little game:

The guns were water pistols, so
Old Bert was drenched from head to toe
In nothing worse than H_2O.

And then the sheriff took a rope,
And skilfully lassoed the dope,
And handed a big bar of soap
To Dirty Cowboy Bert.

Bert had no choice, and so began
To soap himself all over, and
He soon was looking spick and span.

With Cowboy Bert now looking clean,
He didn't seem so big and mean –
Not half the man he once had been.

How they all laughed at Cowboy Bert,
And here's the thing that really hurt –
His nickname soon was *Little Squirt*,
Not Dirty Cowboy Bert.

Hither and Thither

Hither and thither,
She plays on the zither,
Her music is ever so mellow;
But don't stop and dither,
Just look who is with her –
Her husband who's playing the cello.

He scratches and screeches,
The high notes he reaches
Sound more like a cat being sat on;
Conductors throw peaches
When passing, and each is
Soon seen to be breaking his baton.

Both crotchet and quaver
Seem somehow to savour
A key neither major nor minor,
And if I were braver,
I'd ask him a favour,
"Why *don't* you please practise in China?"

Rodney Reid

In his bathtub Rodney Reid is
Making quite a mess,
Thus disproving Archimedes'
Principle,* no less.

(Note the body in this case is
But a boy of four,
Yet the fluid it displaces
Covers all the floor.)

* When a body is immersed in water, its apparent loss of weight is equal to the weight
of the water displaced. So there!

The Unlikely Mermaid

Please pardon my asking you, Irene,
But why do you sit on the stair,
As seaward you gaze out the window
As though there were somebody there?

    The ocean is calling me
    For to return,
    For I was a mermaid
    Before you were born.

Please pardon my ignorance, Irene,
I must seem remarkably dim.
I don't understand – *you* a mermaid?
I know for a fact you can't swim.

A mermaid does many things
Other than float,
Like singing a shanty
By clearing her throat.

Please pardon my doubting you, Irene,
I cannot believe what you say.
Your skin hasn't scales and your body
Resembles a fish in no way.

I wouldn't expect you to
Think it is true;
For I'm not a fire-breathing
Dragon like you.

Humphrey Hughes of Highbury

Young Humphrey Hughes of Highbury
Goes to his local library;
They stamp his books, he softly speaks,
"I'll bring them back within three weeks."
He always looks so meek and mild
That grown-ups think, "There goes a child
Who'll grow into a charming youth."
But little do they know the truth.

For when he's home, young Humphrey Hughes
Forgets to ever wipe his shoes,
And at his mother merely sneers
As to his room he disappears.
When there his library books he takes,
His body with excitement shakes,
For Humphrey so enjoys himself
When placing books upon his shelf.

But there upon his shelf they stay,
Untouched, unread, until the day
He takes one down and with a grin

Looks at the date that's stamped within.
With laughter he begins to shriek,
For all his books were due last week.
He then decides the thing to do
Is wait another week or two.

So time goes by until, at last,
When six or seven weeks have passed,
There comes the knock upon the door
That Humphrey has been waiting for.
His mother gets a nasty shock
When answering the caller's knock,
For there she finds two boys in blue –
In search of books long overdue.

But, pleading absentmindedness,
Young Hughes could simply not care less,
And so, with some reluctancy,
The constables accept his plea.
They take the long-lost books away,
But warn he'll have a fine to pay,
Yet Humphrey merely looks benign,
For Mummy always pays the fine!

I've Lost my Car!

"I've lost my car, I've lost my car,
It's nowhere to be seen!
I've lost my car, I've lost my car,
And it was red and green!"

"I've found your car, I've found your car,
Outside the barber's shop!
I've found your car, I've found your car,
I am a clever cop!"

"A clever cop? Don't make me laugh,
You've no brains in your head!
The car I lost was red and green,
That car is green and red!"

King Solomon

King
Solomon
was
seldom
sad
when
climbing
up
a
column,
but
when
he
started
sliding
down,
King
Solomon
was
solemn!

Pythagoras

With no hesitation
Pythagoras the Greek
Could solve an equation
That would take me a week!

Diogenes

Diogenes was cynical
And lived inside a tub.
He wasn't clean or clinical,
And seldom did he scrub.

He felt no need to wander off
Or visit anyone,
But once told Alexander off
For blocking out the sun.

Archimedes

When Archimedes cried "Eureka!"
And leapt out of his bath,
The people sighed, "Another streaker!"
And kept out of his path.

Nero

Nero, plump about the middle,
Played requests upon the fiddle.
The most engaging tune he played
Was for the local fire brigade.

Boadicea

When Boadicea was on the road,
She didn't heed the Highway Code,
And if she met a Roman crew
Cried, "Fancy running into you!"

Alfred the Great

Alfred the Great was a hero,
But heroes can still make mistakes.
He didn't watch fires like Nero,
And ended up burning the cakes.

King Arthur's Knights

King Arthur's knights were chivalrous
When sat around his table,
But even they were frivolous
Whenever they were able,
And in the moat at Camelot
They splashed about and swam a lot.

Columbus

Columbus very well knew that
The world was round, it wasn't flat,
And almost went hysterical
Just proving it was spherical.

Elizabeth I

Elizabeth the First, I hear,
Was quite a fussy queen,
And had a hot bath once a year
To keep her body clean.

Raleigh and Elizabeth

When Raleigh met Elizabeth,
And it was rather muddy,
He wouldn't let her feet get wet,
He *was* a fuddy-duddy.

So he laid down his velvet cloak,
The Queen, she didn't falter.
She thought it odd, but on it trod,
And said, "Arise, Sir Walter."

Sir Isaac Newton

Sir Isaac Newton liked to grapple
With problems astronomical.
Then on his head there fell an apple,
Which may strike you as comical.
But for Sir Isaac 'twas to be
A matter of some gravity.

Ivan the Terrible

Ivan the Terrible,
The first Russian Tsar,
Was just about bearable,
Till he went too far.

Napoleon

Napoleon Bonaparte
Was never alone, apart
From when he'd tell his queen:
"Not tonight, Josephine."

Charles Blondin

Do you think that Charles Blondin
Practised over a pond in
Preparing to stagger a-
cross Niagara?

George Washington

George Washington chopped down a tree
And couldn't tell a lie;
When questioned by his father, he
Confessed, "Yes, it was I."

But as he handed back the axe,
He added in defence:
"Good training, sir, for lumberjacks
Or would-be presidents."

Einstein

Long years ago, nobody cared
That E was really mc^2.
Then Albert Einstein thought a bit,
And felt that he should mention it.

Stories in Stanzas

Candlestick Hall

I went to a party
At Candlestick Hall:
The spooks and the spectres
Were having a ball.
The hostess, a ghostess,
She was, I am sure –
I noticed the moment
She walked through the door.

The Three Highwaymen

In Hampstead lived three highwaymen
As haughty as could be,
And as to who was handsomest,
They never would agree,
For each one thought, "The prettiest
Undoubtedly is *me!*"

Said Sam, "I have a noble nose
That makes me look refined!"
Said Sid, "My flowing flaxen hair
Leaves all the rest behind!"
Said Saul, "No, it's my sparkling eyes –
They're of the wondrous kind!"

In Hampstead thus the ruffians,
They bickered day and night,
Until at last they all agreed
To find out who was right:
They planned the hold-up of a coach,
Quite soon, in broad daylight;

And furthermore, they all agreed,
To make complete the task,
When having robbed the passengers,
They'd each remove their mask.
Then, "Who's the handsomest of all?"
The passengers they'd ask.

Thought Sam, "They'll see my noble nose
And say I'm so refined!"

Thought Sid, "They'll see my flaxen hair,
That leaves the rest behind!"

Thought Saul, "They'll see my sparkling eyes
Are of the wondrous kind!"

And so it was on Saturday,
Ten minutes after noon,
They stopped a coach on Hampstead Heath

And plundered from it soon;
Then as they each pulled off their mask,
Oh, how the folk did swoon!

The highwaymen were quite perplexed
To see the people faint,
But thought, "It must be ecstasy,
The cause of this complaint.
We all three must be beautiful!"
They laughed without restraint.

And satisfied, they galloped home,
Where they spent several days
Gazing in the mirror through
A sort of rosy haze,
And flattering each other too,
With tender words of praise.

But posters soon were pasted up
Enquiring, *Have you seen*
Three highwaymen – one with a nose
Shaped like a runner bean,
Another who has haystack hair,
And one whose eyes look mean?

The Lighthouse Keeper

I met the lighthouse
keeper's wife,
His nephew, niece,
and daughter;
His uncle and his
auntie too,
When I went 'cross
the water.

I met the lighthouse
keeper's son,
His father and his
mother;
His grandpa and his
grandma too,
His sister and his
brother.

I met the lighthouse
keeper's mate,
Who, running out
of patience,
Told me, "The keeper's
gone ashore
To round up more
relations."

Tom

N.B. To read this poem, be like Tom, and start at the bottom and work your way up!

Divinity.
a Doctor of
and was soon
he spoke with angels
Infinity:
and vanished in
one afternoon
Tom climbed its stalk
its gratitude.
as if to show
ENORMOUS height
it grew to an
a platitude –
with most polite
both day and night
He greeted it
aluminium.
a can of
with water from
and nurtured it
delphinium,
once grew a fine
whose name was Tom
A gardener

My Sister is Missing

Harriet, Harriet, jump on your chariot,
My sister is missing, poor Janet!
And Michael, O Michael, go pedal your cycle,
And search every part of the planet.

My sister, my sister, since breakfast I've missed her,
I'll never grow used to the silence;
So Cecil, O Cecil, I'm glad you can wrestle,
For Janet is prone to use violence.

With Doris and Maurice and Horace and Boris
We'll follow the points of the compass,
And if we should find her, we'll creep up behind her,
But quietly, for Janet might thump us.

We'll hold her and scold her until we have told her
That running away isn't funny;
But if she says sorry, we'll hire a big lorry,
And drive off to somewhere that's sunny.

We'll wander and ponder in fields over yonder,
But wait! What's that dot in the distance?
It looks like a figure, it's getting much bigger,
It's shouting at all my assistants.

O Janet, my Janet, it can't be, or can it?
My sister is no longer missing!
Hooray! We have found her, let's gather around her,
Let's start all the hugging and kissing!

Charlie's Cherry Tree

Every summer Charlie waited
By his Cherry Tree;
Cherries grew and Charlie picked them,
Had them for his tea.

When one summer Charlie waited,
Cherries didn't grow;
Charlie waited for a long time,
Cherries didn't show.

All through summer Charlie waited,
Autumn, winter, spring;
Charlie waited for a whole year,
Didn't get a thing.

Charlie mad and Charlie angry,
Charlie took an axe;
Charlie chopped his Cherry Tree down,
Only took two whacks.

With the wood then Charlie chiselled,
Charlie made a chair;
Now he sits and Charlie wonders
What he's doing there.

Charlie sad and Charlie sorry,
Charlie wishes he
Hadn't been so hasty chopping
Down his Cherry Tree.

Connie and her Unicorn

Early one white winter's morn
Came Connie and her unicorn.
She knocked upon the great front door
Of greedy giant Gobblemore.

The giant, stirring in his bed,
Rubbed both his eyes and scratched his head.
"Who is it dares wake Gobblemore?"
He roared whilst answering the door.
And who should stand there all forlorn,
But Connie and her unicorn.
(Now, though he'd gorged the night before,
He hungered still, did Gobblemore;
Thought he, "Oh, unicorns are sweet,
And how I yearn to eat that meat!")
So, "Dear child, please come in!" he cried.
And thus did Connie go inside.

Her face was thin, her clothes were torn,
But plumpish was her unicorn.
"Dear child, what have you come here for?"
Asked the sly giant, Gobblemore.
(And as he spoke, he noticed that
Her unicorn was nice and fat!)
"Oh sir, I'm sorry," Connie said,
"I come to beg a crust of bread.
I have no money, but I trust
You'll let me have a little crust."
Said Gobblemore (who wasn't kind
And had but one thought in his mind):
"If you've no gold to pay the debt,
Just let me have that freakish pet!"

At such a thought the girl felt sad –
Her unicorn was all she had –
But as she hung her head in woe,
She saw she had no choice, and so
Although her heart was sadly torn,
She sighed, "Farewell, my unicorn."
And with these words, she swapped her beast
For one extremely frugal feast –
Her crust of bread was far from large
And spread with just the merest marge.

Meanwhile, the giant scoured a book
To see the nicest way to cook
A unicorn: fried, boiled or stewed,
Or grilled or baked or barbecued?

When Connie saw the giant take
Her unicorn away to bake,
She realized at once his aim
And thought she'd try to stop his game.
She grabbed a saucepan from a shelf
And closed her eyes and braced herself,
Then flung it, hardly thinking that
She'd hit him, but she knocked him flat!

With Gobblemore now out stone cold,
Shy Connie was a bit more bold:
She dragged the giant round the floor
And kicked him out his own back door,
Then pushed him to the icy well,
And made quite sure that in he fell.

Then with her unicorn she went
And raided his establishment:
They ate up all that they could find
And didn't leave a scrap behind –
Ate every leg of beef and ham,
And every slice of bread and jam,
And every beetroot, every bean –
They even licked their platters clean.
And every goblet, every cup,
They drank them down and drank them up.

It took all day and half the night
To eat up everything in sight,
And when at last they both were sure
There really wasn't any more,
They left, full up, at crack of dawn,
Did Connie and her unicorn.

In Monster Town

The rain came down in Monster Town
And trickled down the drain;
Two Monsters sat on Platform One
And waited for a train.

Said Monster Boy to Monster Girl,
"Your feet I so admire,
Your Monster Toes, they seem to set
My Monster Nose on fire.

"And under your umbrella here,
You make me feel so snug,
Pray take me to your Monster Heart,
Let's have a Monster Hug!"

And so they squeezed
   each other tight,
The way that Monsters do,
Till all their Monster Teeth
   were black,
And all their bones were blue.

Then Monster Girl
   to Monster Boy
Cried, "Hark! Here
   comes the train."
As rain came down
   in Monster Town
And trickled down the drain.

Martha's Hair

In January Martha's hair
Was like the wild mane of a mare.
In February Martha thought
Just for a change she'd cut it short.

In March my Martha dyed it red
And stacked it high upon her head.
In April Martha changed her mind
And wore a pony tail behind.

Come May she couldn't care a fig
And shaved her head and wore a wig.
In June, when it had grown once more,
A yellow ribbon Martha wore.

And in July, like other girls,
My Martha was a mass of curls.
In August, having tired of that,
She combed it out and brushed it flat.

September saw my Martha's hair
With streaks of silver here and there.
And in October, just for fun,
On top she tied it in a bun.

November Martha chose to spend
Making her hair stand up on end.
And by December, Martha's mane
Had grown unruly once again.

Some Stuff in a Sack

One summer's day at half past three
Old Ginger Tom went off to sea,
With some stuff in a sack,
And a parrot called Jack,
Sing Fiddle-dee-fiddle-dee-dee.

Beneath the sun he dozed a while,
Then woke up by a desert isle,
With some stuff in a sack,
Like two boots big and black,
And a parrot called Jack,
Sing Fiddle-dee-fiddle-dee-dee.

He crossed a jungle dark and dim
And nothing seemed to bother him,
With some stuff in a sack,
Like a drum he could whack,
And a parrot called Jack,
Sing Fiddle-dee-fiddle-dee-dee.

He gathered wood beside a lake
And built a fire and took a break,
With some stuff in a sack,
Like a fish finger snack,
And a parrot called Jack,
Sing Fiddle-dee-fiddle-dee-dee.

He met a fearsome pirate crew
But knew exactly what to do,
With some stuff in a sack,
Like a whip that went crack,
And a parrot called Jack,
Sing Fiddle-dee-fiddle-dee-dee.

And then he walked along the shore
And thought he'd put to sea once more,
With some stuff in a sack,
Like a map to get back,
And a parrot called Jack,
Sing Fiddle-dee-fiddle-dee-dee.

And when there came a mighty storm,
Old Ginger Tom slept snug and warm
With some stuff in a sack,
Like a waterproof mac,
And a parrot called Jack,
Sing Fiddle-dee-fiddle-dee-dee.

He woke up when the storm had passed
And saw that he was home at last,
With no stuff in the sack,
(Nothing left to unpack),
Sing Fiddle-dee-fiddle-dee-dee.

And all next day the tale he told
Of Tom's Adventures, Brave and Bold
With some stuff in a sack,
Like two boots big and black,
And a drum he could whack,
And a fish finger snack,
And a whip that went crack,
And a map to get back,
And a waterproof mac,
But that parrot called Jack
Sang: FIDDLE-DEE-FIDDLE-DEE-DEE!

The Saddest Spook

The saddest spook there ever was
Is melancholious because
He can't so much as raise a sneer,
Or laugh a laugh that's vaguely queer.

He hasn't learnt to walk through walls,
And dares not answer wolfish calls,
And when big ghosts are rude and coarse,
And shout at him: "Your fangs are false,"

He smiles at them, just like a fool,
But wishes they'd pick on a ghoul
Who's heavyweight and not just bantam,
Why pick on a little phantom?

Rolling Down a Hill

I'm rolling
rolling
rolling
down

I'm rolling
down a
hill.
down
rolling
rolling
down

I'm rolling
rolling
rolling
down it still.

I'm rolling
down it still.

I'm rolling
rolling
rolling
down

I'm rolling
down a
hill.

I'm rolling
rolling
rolling
down

But now
I'm feeling
ill.

Park Regulations

The rules upon this board displayed
Are here by all to be obeyed:

Keep off the grass. Don't scale the wall.
Don't throw, or kick, or bat a ball.
Don't pluck the flowers from their bed.
Don't feed the ducks with crusts of bread.
Bicycles may not be ridden.
Rollerskating is forbidden.
Dogs must be kept upon their leashes
And kept from chasing other species.
Dispose of litter thoughtfully.
Do not attempt to climb a tree
Or carve initials on the bark.
Don't play a wireless in the park
(Or any sort of instrument).
Don't build a fire or pitch a tent
And don't throw stones or gather sticks.
The gates are closed at half past six.

Observe these rules and regulations
(Signed) Head of Parks and Recreations.

Grandfather Clock

O grandfather clock, dear old grandfather clock,
How charming to hear is your tick and your tock;
So upright you stand day and night in the hall,
Your feet on the ground and your back to the wall.
Although I may grumble most mornings at
    eight,
When you chime, "Hurry up, or you're
    bound to be late,"
I'm grateful to greet you at five o'clock
    when
You chime, "Welcome home, nice to
    see you again."
I think it is thoughtless when relatives
    speak
And rudely refer to you as an antique;
It also seems heartless when sometimes
    they say
You'd fetch a fair price at an auction
    one day.
I know that you're old and inclined to
    be slow,
But I hope that they never decide you
    should go.
How dull life would be if they took
    you away:
You give me much more than the time
    of the day.

I'll be in the Wardrobe, Wilma

I'll be in the wardrobe, Wilma,
If you should ever call,
Or putting up a chandelier,
Or papering a wall.

And I'll be too tired to answer,
If you should ever phone,
And, Wilma, though it grieves me so,
I need to be alone.

I'll be up the chimney, Wilma,
If you should ever write,
Too busy to reply to you,
I'm up there day and night.

But if you *should* bump into me
One day when I'm off-guard,
I'll say, "You must drop in some time,
Sweet Wilma, here's my card!"

U.F.O.

A UFO, a UFO,
have you ever
seen a UFO?

Yes, I've seen a UFO –
an Ugly Frog Ogling
a rather pretty crow.

A UFO, a UFO,
have you ever
seen a UFO?

Yes, I've seen a UFO –
an Uncouth Fellow, Oswald,
not very nice to know.

A UFO, a UFO,
have you ever
seen a UFO?

Yes, I've seen a UFO –
an Ultra Friendly Ox
gave me a lift to Stow.

A UFO, a UFO,
have you ever
seen a UFO?

Yes, I've seen a UFO –
an Understanding Freckled Owl,
whose voice was soft and low.

A UFO, a UFO,
have you ever
seen a UFO?

Yes, I've seen a UFO –
an Unbelieving Foolish Oaf
I met not long ago.

A UFO, a UFO,
you've never
seen a UFO!

But I have, I have,
I'll have you know,
it's back to Venus, Earthling,
in my spaceship,
cheerio!

Jeremiah

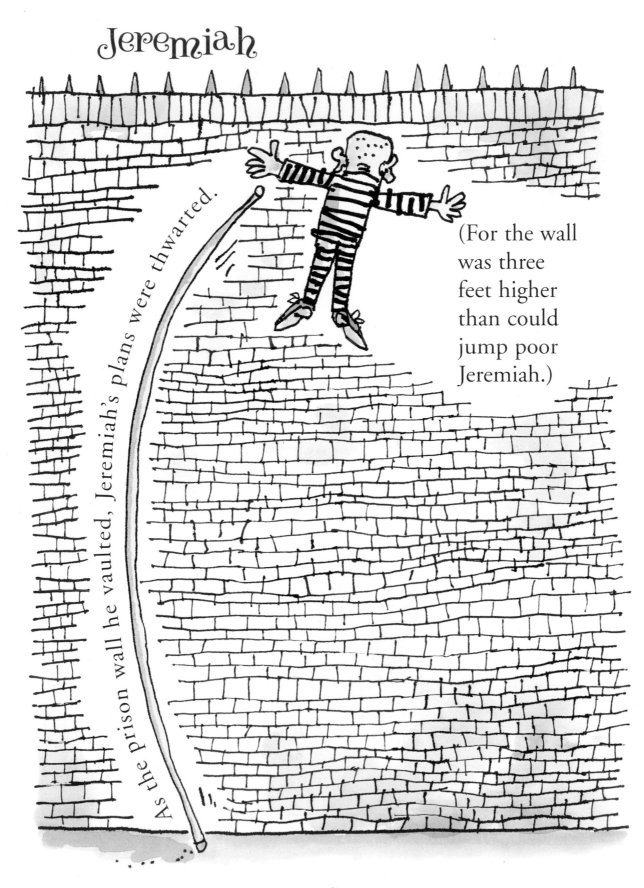

As the prison wall he vaulted, Jeremiah's plans were thwarted.

(For the wall was three feet higher than could jump poor Jeremiah.)

Trevor is Ever so

Trevor is ever so clever,
Trevor is ever so clean,
Trevor is welcome wherever
Trevor is heard or is seen.

Trevor is ever so handsome,
Trevor is ever so nice,
Trevor is worth any ransom,
Trevor is worth any price.

Trevor is ever so charming,
Trevor is ever so sweet,
Trevor is never alarming,
Trevor is truly a treat.

Trevor is ever so youthful,
Trevor is ever so bright,
Trevor is ever so truthful,
Trevor is very polite.

Trevor is ever so modest,
Trevor, oh how do I know?
Trevor, the thing I find oddest:
Trevor *alone* told me so.

Wobble-dee-woo

What would you do
With a Wobble-dee-woo?
Would you eat it
Or wear it
Or play it?
What would you do
With a Wobble-dee-woo?
(I've only just learned
How to say it.)

What would you do
With a Wobble-dee-woo?
Would you wear it
Or play it
Or eat it?
What would you do
With a Wobble-dee-woo?
(I'm sorry, I'll have
To repeat it.)

What would you do
With a Wobble-dee-woo?
Would you play it
Or eat it
Or wear it?
What would you do
With a Wobble-dee-woo?
(It's driving me mad,
I can't bear it!)

Crocodile or Alligator?

Crocodile or alligator,
Who is who on the equator?
Which one ate up Auntie Norah,
Famous tropical explorer?

Cool she was and calm she kept, I'll
Bet you that repulsive reptile
Had a hard job as he ate her,
Crocodile *or* alligator.

Norah, sister of my mother,
Couldn't tell one from the other;
Had she only read this fable,
Maybe she'd have then been able.

Crocodiles, with jaws shut tightly,
Show their teeth off impolitely;
But alligators aren't so rude,
And seldom let their teeth protrude.

Whether former, whether latter,
To Aunt Norah doesn't matter;
She's at rest inside his tummy,
What a dinner, yummy, yummy!

As I went down to Milton Keynes

As I went down to Milton Keynes,
I met a king with seven queens;
For every queen there was a prince,
For every prince, a princess fair,
For every princess fair, an earl,
For every earl, there was a lady,
For every lady, there was a baby,
For every baby, there was a cat,
Now, how many do you make of that?

Hang on – I'll process the data
When I find my calculator.

Nuts

Fred said:
"Hey, I'm nuts about nuts!"

"What sort of nuts?"
Asked Sam.

Fred said:
"Peanuts and walnuts,
Cashew nuts, all nuts!
Pecan nuts, hazel nuts,
All day long I praise all nuts!
Nuts, nuts, nuts,
Yeah, I'm just NUTS about nuts!"

Sam said:
"Well, I am …
Bananas about bananas!"

"What sort of bananas?"
Asked Fred.

"What sort ?"
Said Sam,
"Well, bananas,"
Said Sam,
"Just, bananas."

Barge Pole

Poetry?
I wouldn't touch it with a barge pole.

Well,
How about:
A long pole,
A lean pole,
A bamboo or
A bean pole?
A flag pole,
A tent pole,
A barber's or
A bent pole?
A green pole,
A grey pole,
A curtain or
A maypole?
A whole pole,
A half pole,
A great big
Telegraph pole?

No!
Not any sort –
No small pole,
No large pole –
I wouldn't touch it with a barge pole.

Etymology for Entomologists

O Longitude and Latitude,
I always get them muddled;
(I'm sure they'd be offended, though,
To think that I'm befuddled).

O Isobars and Isotherms,
Please tell me how they differ;
(For competition 'twixt the two,
I hear, could not be stiffer).

O Seraphim and Cherubim,
Don't care for one another;
(Although for me it's difficult
To tell one from the other).

O Stalagmites and Stalactites,
Whenever I peruse 'em,
Though one grows up, and one grows down,
I can't help but confuse 'em.

Have You Ever?

Have
you
ever
perched
a
poem
on
your
nose?

Have you
ever worn
a verse
upon your
clothes?

Have you ever sniffed a sonnet in a rose?

Have you ever

    caught a

      rhyme

       before   it   goes?

A Hat

I'm going to the hatter
For to purchase me a hat.
It doesn't really matter
If it's tall or if it's flat.

I don't mind if it's black or brown,
Or if it has a crumpled crown,
Or if the brim is up or down;
A simple hat is all I ask,
To cover up my ears.

I don't ask for a bonnet
That is made of velveteen,
With a lot of ribbons on it
That are yellow, pink or green.

I don't ask for a hat of crêpe,
Or one of an exotic shape,
Or one that's all tied up with tape;
A simple hat is all I ask,
To cover up my ears.

I don't want one with feathers,
Or with cherries ripe and red,
A plain hat for all weathers
Would be fine for me instead.

I do not really mind a bit
If my hat's not a *perfect* fit,
If I can just get into it,
A simple hat is all I ask,
To cover up my ears.

Old Song Revisited

It was a feline fiddler
Who played a merry tune
Inspired a bovine acrobat
To leap over the moon;
A canine witness was amused
At shows of such buffoon-
Ery; a piece of crockery
Eloped with what? A spoon!

Leaflets

Leaflets, leaflets, I like leaflets,
I love leaflets when they're free.
When I see a pile of leaflets,
I take one, or two (or three).

Banks are always good for leaflets –
They've got lots of leaflets there –
Leaflets on investing money:
How to be a Millionaire.

And I go to my Gas Show Room,
For their leaflets are such fun,
And I visit travel agents –
They've got leaflets by the ton.

Leaflets, leaflets, I like leaflets,
I love leaflets when they're free.
When I see a pile of leaflets,
Something strange comes over me.

Theatre foyers offer leaflets:
What to see and how to book.
Stations, libraries and so on –
All have leaflets if you look.

I've got leaflets by the dozen,
I've got leaflets by the score,
I've got leaflets by the hundred,
Yet I always yearn for more.

Ask a Silly Question

Tell me how in the deep
Does the whale go to sleep,
How does he rest his poor blubber?

He lays down his head
Upon the sea bed,
And snores just like a landlubber!

Tell me why in the sky
Can an ostrich not fly,
Why can't he fly like an eagle?

Because he once heard
From some funny bird
That flying is highly illegal!

Tell me where on the earth
Does the monkey find mirth,
Where does he go to find laughter?

He climbs up a tree
To watch you and me,
Then happily lives ever after!

Jocelyn, My Dragon

My dragon's name is Jocelyn,
He's something of a joke.
For Jocelyn is very tame,
He doesn't like to maul or maim,
Or breathe a fearsome fiery flame;
He's much too smart to smoke.

And when I take him to the park
The children form a queue,
And say, "What lovely eyes of red!"
As one by one they pat his head.
And Jocelyn is so well-bred,
He only eats a few!

The Bridle and the Saddle

The bridle and the saddle
Fitted, I sit in the middle
Of the horse, but why I straddle
Such a creature is a riddle.

O, he's big and I am little,
And he no doubt thinks I'm idle,
And he knows my bones be brittle
As I hang on to the bridle.

But it doesn't seem to addle
Him that I am in a muddle
As I cower in the saddle
When we pass over each puddle.

Don't Look in the Mirror, Maud

O, don't look in the mirror, Maud,
I fear that you might crack it.
A new one I could not afford,
Unless I sold my jacket.

And if I sold my jacket, Maud,
I could no longer wear it;
And then I couldn't go abroad –
I'm sure I couldn't bear it.

For if I couldn't travel, Maud,
I'd never go to Venice;
I'd have to stay behind with Claud,
And practise playing tennis.

And if he were to ask me, Maud,
If we could play mixed doubles,
He'd thereby contribute toward
My many other troubles.

For if we played mixed doubles, Maud,
With Vivian and Vera,
They'd dress me up just like a lord
Before that very mirror.

And if 'twere broke, they'd be appalled,
And hit me with my racket;
So don't look in the mirror, Maud,
I fear that you might crack it.

Socks

My local Gents' Outfitter stocks
The latest line in snazzy socks:
Black socks, white socks,
Morning, noon and night socks,
Grey socks, green socks,
Small, large and in between socks,
Blue socks, brown socks,
Always-falling-down socks,
Orange socks, red socks,
Baby socks and bed socks;
Purple socks, pink socks,
What-would-people-think socks,
Holey socks and frayed socks,
British Empire-made socks,
Long socks, short socks,
Any-sort-of-sport socks,
Thick socks, thin socks,
And "these-have-just-come-in" socks.

Socks with stripes and socks with spots,
Socks with stars and polka dots,
Socks for ankles, socks for knees,
Socks with twelve-month guarantees,
Socks for aunties, socks for uncles,
Socks to cure you of carbuncles,
Socks for nephews, socks for nieces,
Socks that won't show up their creases,
Socks whose colour glows fluorescent,
Socks for child or adolescent,

Socks for ladies, socks for gents,
Socks for only fifty pence.

Socks for winter, socks for autumn,
Socks with garters to support 'em,
Socks for work and socks for leisure,
Socks hand-knitted, made-to-measure,
Socks of wool and polyester,
Socks from Lincoln, Leeds and Leicester,
Socks of cotton and elastic,
Socks of paper, socks of plastic,
Socks of silk-embroidered satin,
Socks with mottoes done in Latin,
Socks for soldiers in the army,
Socks to crochet or macramé,
Socks for destinations distant,
Shrink-proof, stretch-proof, heat-resistant.

Baggy socks, brief socks,
Union Jack motif socks,
Chequered socks, tartan socks,
School or kindergarten socks,
Sensible socks, silly socks,
Frivolous and frilly socks,
Impractical socks, impossible socks,
Drip-dry machine-only-washable socks,
Bulgarian socks, Brazilian socks,
There seem to be over a million socks!

With all these socks, there's just one catch –
It's hard to find a pair that match.

Flying Pizzas from Outer Space

Pizzas are coming from Outer Space,
They're flying and falling all over the place,
They float on the breeze and zoom over trees,
Then land with a SPLAT in my face.

Pizzas from Pluto,
Pizzas from Mars,
With cheese from the Moon
And dust from the stars.

I've had a whole heap of these pizzas,
Pizzas that fall from the sky,
Pizzas that hover and quiver,
Then land with a WHACK in my eye.

Pizzas from Venus,
Pizzas from Mars,
With Jupiter toppings
And dust from the stars.

One day I may open a parlour
That serves up these pizzas from Space
Till then I'll just eat them whenever
They land with a PLOP in my face.

Pizzas from Saturn,
Pizzas from Mars,
With Mercury pastry
And dust from the stars.

Z

I know a place called Zagazig.
I can't live there, it's much too big.

I know a place called Zyradow.
I lived there once, I don't know how.

I know a place called Zanzibar.
I can't go there, it's much too far.

I know a place called Zonguldak.
I went there once – I won't go back.

I know a place called Zhitomir.
I can't think why I'm staying here.

I know a place called Zug. I thought
I'd go there as a last resort …

The End

PS With many thanks to Caroline,
For dreaming up this book of mine.